Dear Parent:

Congratulations! Your child is taking the first steps on an exciting journey. The destination? Independent reading!

STEP INTO READING® will help your child get there. The program offers five steps to reading success. Each step includes fun stories and colorful art. There are also Step into Reading Sticker Books, Step into Reading Math Readers, Step into Reading Write-In Readers, Step into Reading Phonics Readers, and Step into Reading Phonics First Steps! Boxed Sets—a complete literacy program with something for every child.

Learning to Read, Step by Step!

Ready to Read Preschool–Kindergarten
• big type and easy words • rhyme and rhythm • picture clues
For children who know the alphabet and are eager to begin reading.

Reading with Help Preschool–Grade 1
• basic vocabulary • short sentences • simple stories
For children who recognize familiar words and sound out new words with help.

Reading on Your Own Grades 1–3
• engaging characters • easy-to-follow plots • popular topics
For children who are ready to read on their own.

Reading Paragraphs Grades 2–3
• challenging vocabulary • short paragraphs • exciting stories
For newly independent readers who read simple sentences with confidence.

Ready for Chapters Grades 2–4
• chapters • longer paragraphs • full-color art
For children who want to take the plunge into chapter books but still like colorful pictures.

STEP INTO READING® is designed to give every child a successful reading experience. The grade levels are only guides. Children can progress through the steps at their own speed, developing confidence in their reading, no matter what their grade.

Remember, a lifetime love of reading starts with a single step!

For Ramona and Leo—A.J.

Step into Reading, Random House, and the Random House colophon are registered trademarks of Random House, Inc.

Visit us on the Web!
www.stepintoreading.com
www.randomhouse.com/kids/disney

Educators and librarians, for a variety of teaching tools, visit us at
www.randomhouse.com/teachers

Library of Congress Cataloging-in-Publication Data
Jordan, Apple.
Love at first beep / by Apple Jordan. — 1st ed.
    p. cm. — (Step into reading. Step 2 book)
Summary: WALL•E, a lonely robot, falls in love with EVE, who has come to Earth looking for plant life to take back to her ship, and after she sees how WALL•E cares for her, she falls in love with him too.
    ISBN: 978-0-7364-2514-8 (trade)
    ISBN: 978-0-7364-8057-4 (lib. ed.)
[1. Robots—Fiction. 2. Science fiction.]
I. Title.
PZ7.J755 Lo 2008   [E]—dc22   2007041694

Printed in the United States of America   10 9   First Edition

DISNEY · PIXAR

WALL·E

LOVE AT FIRST BEEP

By Apple Jordan
Illustrated by Caroline Egan, Seung Lee Kim,
Elizabeth Tate, and Scott Tilley
Painted by Maria Elena Naggi, Mara Damiani,
Andrea Cagol, and Giorgio Vallorani
Inspired by the art and character designs created by Pixar

Random House 🏠 New York

WALL·E was a robot.

He lived all alone

on Earth.

He spent his days
stacking trash.
But WALL•E wanted
to do more.

WALL•E was made
of metal.
But he had
a big heart.

He knew about love.
He had learned
about it from a movie.

WALL•E found
many nice things
in the trash.
He found a living plant.

He had never
seen one before.
Plants no longer grew
on his planet.

One day,
a spaceship landed.
A pretty, shiny
robot came out.

It was love
at first sight
for WALL•E.

The new robot did not
know about love.
She just had
a job to do.

She had to find life
on the planet.

WALL·E asked the robot
her name.
"EVE,"
she said.

"Eee-vah!"

WALL•E cried.

He wanted

to show her everything.

WALL·E showed his
things to EVE.
EVE liked WALL·E.

WALL•E was happy.

He was not lonely

anymore.

WALL·E showed
EVE his plant.
She grabbed it from him.
Then she shut down.

She had found life.

Her job was done.

WALL·E was confused.

WALL•E tried
to wake EVE up.
It was no use.
So he cared for EVE
while she slept.

He took her
for a boat ride.

He kept her dry
in the rain.

Soon the spaceship
came back for EVE.

WALL•E had to follow
EVE into space.
He was in love!

EVE woke up

on a bigger spaceship.

WALL·E was there, too.
EVE was confused.

EVE saw how WALL•E
had taken care of her.

Now EVE knew
all about love.
She had learned
from WALL•E.

WALL•E and EVE
went back
to Earth.

Love and life
had been growing there
all along.